The Gold Family

By Adam Kownacki

Dedication

To Lilliana K.

Your boldness, creativity, and
love revised my soul and
prepared me for the unknown.

I'm Lilly Gold and I'm going to tell you a story from my childhood. My father was the king of our small village. We lived deep within the vast blue waters. We had always lived in the same place. It was safe and peaceful there and we loved it. I should probably tell you now... we're mermaids.

Where we live, the coral, plants, and colorful rocks are too beautiful to describe. And the water there is the prettiest blue you've ever seen.

One day, my family was playing catch with an ancient red stone, called the love stone. The stone is special. It is a deep red color and is very strong. My grandpa built our castle from the love stone. At family gatherings, we play "love stone catch," like the generations before us.

We were so caught up in the excitement of the game that we didn't notice two bandit fish entering our village. While we played, bandits kidnapped my dad. He was gone. I was crushed. Why didn't I pay better attention? I blamed myself.

My life became dedicated to figuring out who had taken my dad. I began going further and further out into the dark waters. No one else ever did this.

While searching I learned about the shadow bandits. They were the only bandits able to breach our property. Shadow bandits came from the dreaded Doctor Shadow's Fish Zoo. Doctor Shadow kidnapped fish from each generation of the Gold family. This was a dark family secret that no one ever spoke of.

I spent months looking for my dad. Finally, I received a clue from an old shark. He lived outside the rusty gates of the zoo. The shark wanted to meet and he wanted me to pay him for information about my dad.

I had a pocket full of love stones as I set out to meet the old shark. Before I could reach out with my hand to shake his tattered fin, I was shackled and blindfolded. The shark set me up! I was tricked and kidnapped by the same bandit fish that took my dad.

I wasn't scared. I knew I would see my dad and we would plan our escape. I had prepared for months. I was ready for this mission. Even with some uneasy feelings. I was determined. I would bring my father home to his beloved kingdom.

The bandit fish brought me into the zoo and removed my blindfold. I saw hundreds of cages filled with fish. I thought to myself, how could all these fish not join together and overpower the two guards? As I looked around I saw plenty of ways to escape. My mission was clear.

The bandits unlocked a rusty old cage with a golden key. They took all of my love stones and removed my shackles. I was pushed into the cage and the door slammed behind me. The bars on the cage shook the ground and all the other cages. The other fish woke up and looked around, wondering what the commotion was about.

Just then, I saw my dad at the far end of the row. He was the only fish that hadn't gotten up to see what was going on. He just laid in bed watching TV. He didn't even flinch at the noise. He wasn't the same. Something was terribly wrong.

I was discouraged and decided to wait a few days to try and escape. When I slept I had bad dreams about the scary dark waters and the long journey home. The thought of escaping seemed impossible. I thought about giving up.

Every morning the bandits brought me breakfast. Every afternoon a snack and lunch. Then at night, they would bring dinner and tea with dessert.

My bed was comfy and the tablet had all my favorite shows. Maybe I didn't need to leave. This place wasn't so bad.

One night I had a dream about my castle and my family. It was so real. I realized they needed us. The kingdom needed my dad and me! This cage was no way to live. We needed our loved ones too!

The bandits were bringing breakfast. When they opened my cage, the bandit accidentally kicked a love stone in. It rolled in and glistened brightly. I was shocked they didn't see it. Once they left I quickly hid the stone under my arm.

I felt the love stored inside the stone and remembered the joyful moments in my life. The mission to save my dad had been revived!

I noticed that whenever the bandits brought in a new fish and slammed their jail door shut, the vibration would knock pieces of rust off the bars. Being a small kid, I wondered if I could squeeze myself through the bars. The cells were made for bigger fish, not small mermaids. I exhaled all the air out of my lungs, sucked in my stomach, and squeezed through! I made a beeline straight for my dad's cell. He was sleeping and didn't notice me. I went back to my cage to plan.

I tried to convince my dad over the next three days to go home. On the first day, I skipped breakfast so I could squeeze through the bars. I swam straight to my dad's cell, and excitedly said, "Let's go, we can swim back home." My dad, half asleep in his bed, said, "We can't, the bandits will be back to collect breakfast plates." Just then, I heard them coming and I swam as fast as I could. I vowed to try again the next day.

On the second day, I skipped lunch so I could be sure to squeeze through the bars again. I swam to my dad's cell and said, "Let's get out of here, let's go." He said, "The bandits are going to be coming back and we'll be caught." Once again I heard the clamoring of the guards. I rushed back to my cell. I vowed to try again the next day.

On the third day, I decided to try at dinner time. I squeezed through the bars and rushed down to my dad's cell. I told him, "We must go, it will be a long journey home." My dad turned off the TV, turned to me, and said, "The bandit fish will be back to clear our dinner plates, and besides, that journey back home sounds too scary."

I went back to my cell feeling discouraged. My dad is too comfortable in this terrible place. He's been alone for too long. He doesn't want to go home or be a king anymore.

Almost giving up, I pulled the stone out from under my arm. I decided to ask it what I should do. I held the stone tight in my hands and said, "I don't know what to do. What will give my dad the courage to leave?" At that moment, the stone began to hum. Then a vibration grew stronger and stronger. It sounded like the engine of a huge battleship getting ready for war. It rattled all the locks off the cells and the doors sprung open! I knew that my dad needed to touch the stone. Then he would remember the joyful moments of his reign and of being a brave king.

Fish were excitedly leaving their cages. I swam out of mine, through the chaos, and straight to my dad. I swung open his cell door with such force that it knocked it off the hinges. I threw the stone to my dad. As it glided through the water, I could see the spark of the noble king coming back to him. I asked if he was ready to go. He clutched the stone in his hand and said, "Lead us out of here my beautiful daughter!"

I lead him out of the zoo and into the open waters. I quickly figured out which direction was west and remembered I had traveled that way before. "Follow me," I told my dad.

We left the zoo and swam into the dark waters. We swam with purpose knowing the journey was long, but that it would lead us back to our kingdom and the people we love.

The End

Book design, layout, and illustrations by Sherri Marteney.

ISBN 979-8-9879973-0-7 Paperback
ISBN 979-8-9879973-1-4 Ebook